# Octopus

## Judy Wearing

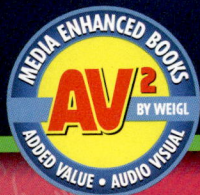

MEDIA ENHANCED BOOKS

AV2 BY WEIGL

ADDED VALUE · AUDIO VISUAL

www.av2books.com

# MEDIA ENHANCED BOOKS

## AV²
### BY WEIGL™
### ADDED VALUE • AUDIO VISUAL

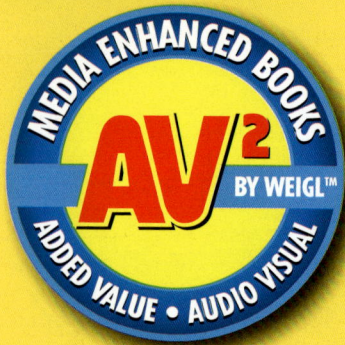

Go to **www.av2books.com**, and enter this book's unique code.

## BOOK CODE

**U 6 8 6 1 6 6**

**AV² by Weigl** brings you media enhanced books that support active learning.

AV² provides enriched content that supplements and complements this book. Weigl's AV² books strive to create inspired learning and engage young minds in a total learning experience.

## Your AV² Media Enhanced books come alive with...

**Audio**
Listen to sections of the book read aloud.

**Video**
Watch informative video clips.

**Embedded Weblinks**
Gain additional information for research.

**Try This!**
Complete activities and hands-on experiments.

**Key Words**
Study vocabulary, and complete a matching word activity.

**Quizzes**
Test your knowledge.

**Slide Show**
View images and captions, and prepare a presentation.

**... and much, much more!**

Published by AV² by Weigl
350 5th Avenue, 59th Floor New York, NY 10118
Website: www.av2books.com    www.weigl.com

Library of Congress Cataloging-in-Publication Data

Wearing, Judy.
 Octopus / Judy Wearing.
   p. cm. -- (Ocean life)
 Includes index.
 ISBN 978-1-61690-689-4 (hardcover : alk. paper) -- ISBN 978-1-61690-693-1 (softcover : alk. paper)
 1. Octopuses--Juvenile literature. I. Title.
 QL430.3.O2W39 2012
 594'.56--dc22
                        2010050417

Printed in the United States of America in North Mankato, Minnesota
1 2 3 4 5 6 7 8 9 0   15 14 13 12 11

**Project Coordinator**: Aaron Carr
**Art Director**: Terry Paulhus

Weigl acknowledges Getty Images, Dreamstime, and Peter Arnold as image suppliers for this title.

**2**

052011
WEP37500

# CONTENTS

# What is an Octopus?

Have you ever seen a sea animal with eight arms? It may have been an octopus. Octopuses live in oceans around the world. They are shaped like a ball, with eight soft arms attached to one end.

Octopuses are related to snails and slugs.

# Soft Squeeze

Can you feel your bones? The octopus does not have bones. Its soft body can squeeze and fold. This allows it to fit into tight spaces between rocks and **coral**.

The octopus uses its soft body to swim. It squeezes water out of a tube called a **siphon**. Pushing water out of the siphon moves the octopus forward.

# An Armful

What would you do if you had eight arms? Octopuses use their arms for many tasks. They use their arms to eat and to **mate**. They also use their arms to build shelters. Octopuses can even open jars with the tips of their arms.

Each octopus arm has one or two rows of round **suckers**. The suckers help the octopus stick to rocks on the ocean floor.

Octopuses taste food with their suckers.

# What's for Dinner?

Did you know that octopuses are **predators**? They use their arms to catch clams, shrimp, lobsters, crabs, and other small sea creatures.

An octopus's mouth is on the bottom of its body. The mouth has a sharp **beak.** The octopus uses this beak to break open the hard shells of its food.

# Getting Away

Have you ever tried to hide from someone? Some octopuses can change color. They do this to match the rocks and coral around them. Changing color helps them hide from predators.

Many octopuses have ink in their bodies. If a predator comes close, they squirt ink into the water. The ink hides the octopus as it escapes.

# Octopus IQ

Did you know octopuses are one of the smartest animals in the ocean? When octopuses hunt, they remember where they are and how to get home.

Octopuses are one of the few animals that can use tools. They pile rocks to make the opening of their **den**. Octopuses also spray water on the inside of their den to keep it clean.

# Smallest to Biggest

Have you ever seen a bus driving down the road? Some octopuses can be almost as long as a bus. The giant Pacific octopus is the largest octopus in the world. The biggest giant Pacific octopus ever found was about 30 feet (9 meters) long.

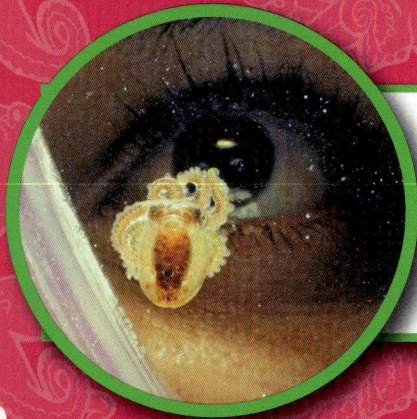

The smallest octopus lives in the Pacific Ocean. It is the size of a dime.

# Pretty but Dangerous

Did you know that some octopuses are **venomous**? The blue-ringed octopus is one of the most deadly animals in the ocean. A person can die from a blue-ringed octopus bite in less than 90 minutes.

When the blue-ringed octopus is afraid, bright blue rings appear on its yellow body and arms. These rings warn enemies to stay away.

The blue-ringed octopus is about the size of a golf ball.

# Baby Bath

Have you ever seen a bird sitting on eggs? Female octopuses also take care of their eggs. The eggs hang in strings from the roof of an octopus den. The mother stays in the den to protect the eggs until they **hatch**.

# Octopus Water Hose

**Supplies**

turkey baster, purple food coloring, sand, two plastic bowls, a large bucket, and water

1. Fill a bucket with water, and place a plastic bowl at the bottom. This is the octopus's den. Put some sand in the den.

2. Hold the turkey baster under the water. Squeeze and release the top to fill it with water. Then, squeeze the water out of the tube. This is how an octopus's siphon works.

3. Pretend to be an octopus cleaning out its den. Spray water with your siphon to clean the sand away. Do you think spraying water works as well as a broom?

4. In the other plastic bowl, mix some food coloring and water to make ink. Then, suck the ink into your baster.

5. Hold the baster in the water. Pretend to be an octopus with a shark coming close. Squeeze the ink out of the siphon.

6. What happens when you squirt ink into the water? How would squirting ink help an octopus escape from a shark?

# Glossary

**beak:** a hard part of the mouth on some animals

**coral:** a hard object in the ocean that is made by a small sea animal

**den:** the shelter and hiding place of an animal

**hatch:** to come out of an egg

**mate:** when a male and female come together to have young

**predators:** animals that hunt other animals for food

**siphon:** a tube that is used to move liquids

**suckers:** rounded hollows that stick to surfaces

**venomous:** able to bite or sting using poison

# Index

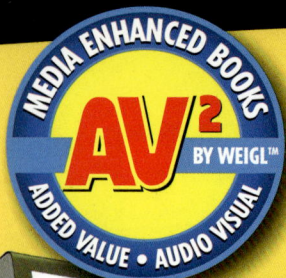

# Log on to www.av2books.com

AV² by Weigl brings you media enhanced books that support active learning. Go to www.av2books.com, and enter the special code found on page 2 of this book. You will gain access to enriched and enhanced content that supplements and complements this book. Content includes video, audio, web links, quizzes, a slide show, and activities.

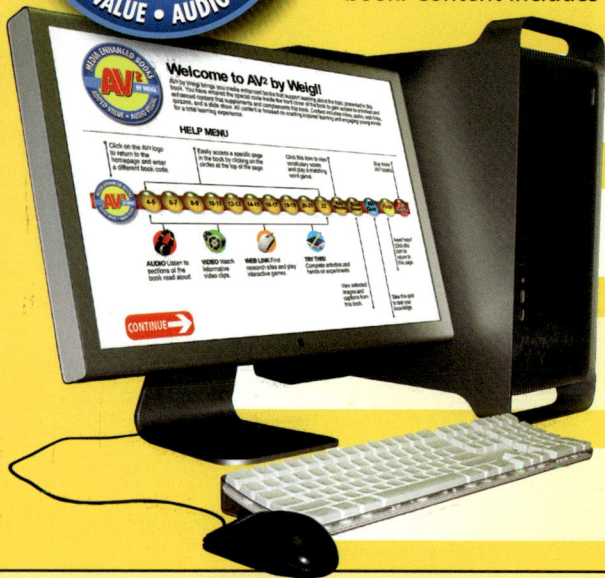

**Audio**
Listen to sections of the book read aloud.

**Video**
Watch informative video clips.

**Embedded Weblinks**
Gain additional information for research.

**Try This!**
Complete activities and hands-on experiments.

# WHAT'S ONLINE?

| Try This! | Embedded Weblinks | Video | EXTRA FEATURES |
|---|---|---|---|
| Gain a better understanding of an octopus's size with this fun comparison activity. | Find out more information on octopuses. | Watch an introductory video on octopuses. | **Audio** Listen to sections of the book read aloud. |
| Identify the benefits of an octopus's defensive adaptations. | Check out myths and legends about octopuses. | Watch a video of an octopus in its natural environment. | **Key Words** Study vocabulary, and complete a matching word activity. |
| Complete a fun coloring activity. | Learn more on an octopus's diet and nutrition. | | **Slide Show** View images and captions, and prepare a presentation. |
| | | | **Quizzes** Test your knowledge. |

AV² was built to bridge the gap between print and digital. We encourage you to tell us what you like and what you want to see in the future. Sign up to be an AV² Ambassador at www.av2books.com/ambassador.

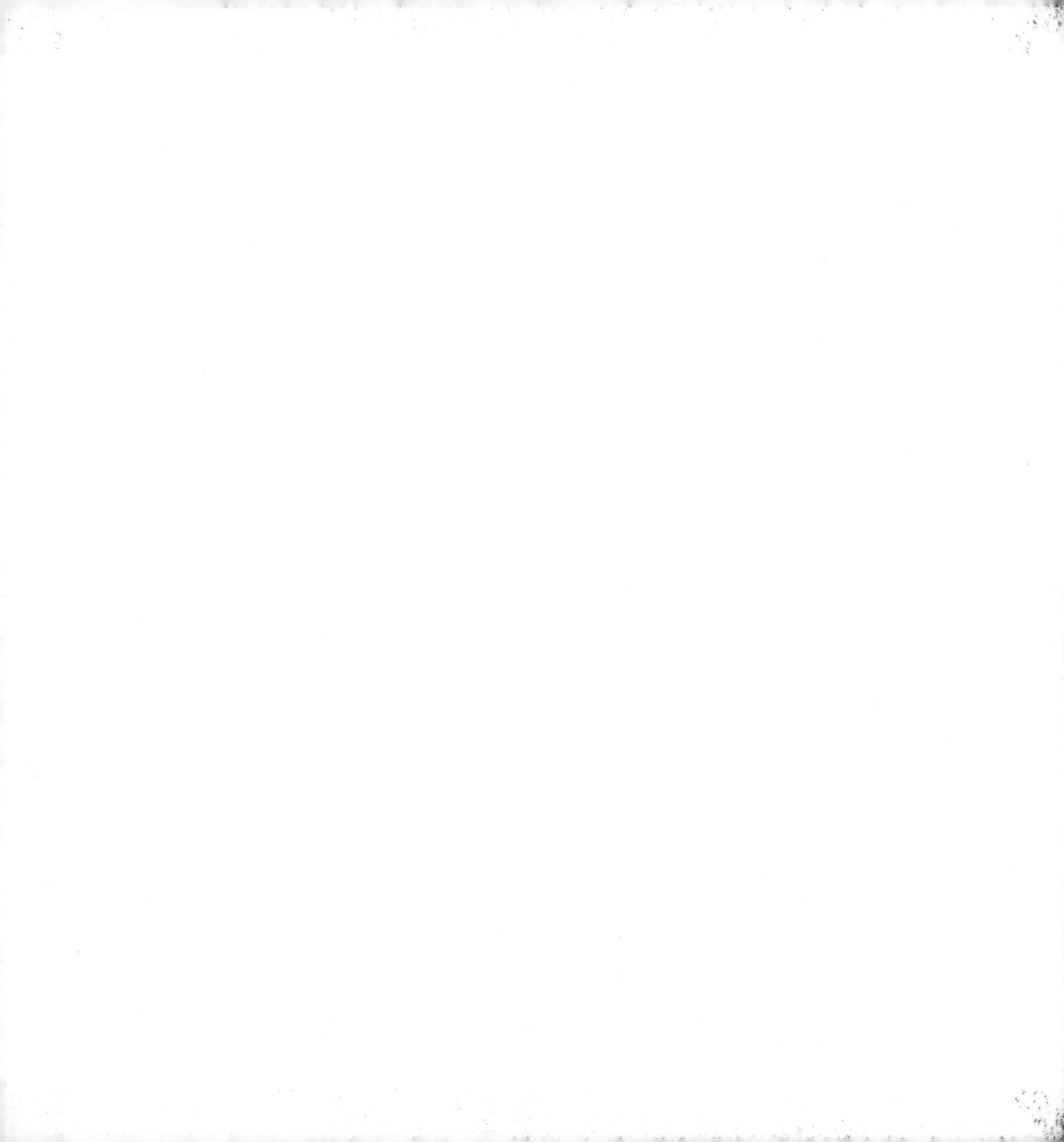